RATTLESNAKE STEW

RATTLESNAKE

LYNN ROWE REED

FARRAR · STRAUS · GIROUX

NEW YORK

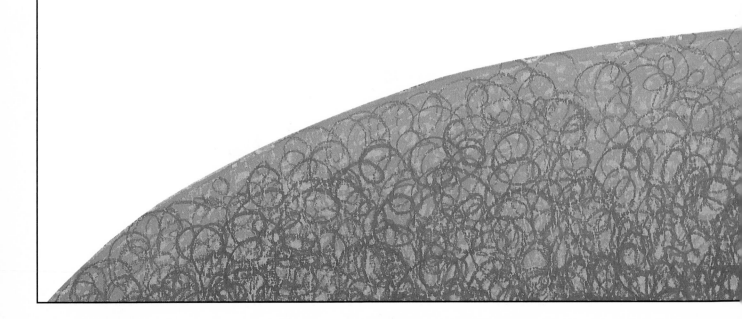

STEW

For Nathaniel
and Anthony

Juvle
fic

Copyright © 1990 by Lynn Rowe Reed
All rights reserved
Library of Congress
catalog card number: 90-55163
Published simultaneously in Canada
by HarperCollins*CanadaLtd*
Printed and bound
in the United States of America
by Horowitz/Rae Book Manufacturers
Designed by Martha Rago
First edition, 1990

A strong wind swirled and soared and whirled and roared

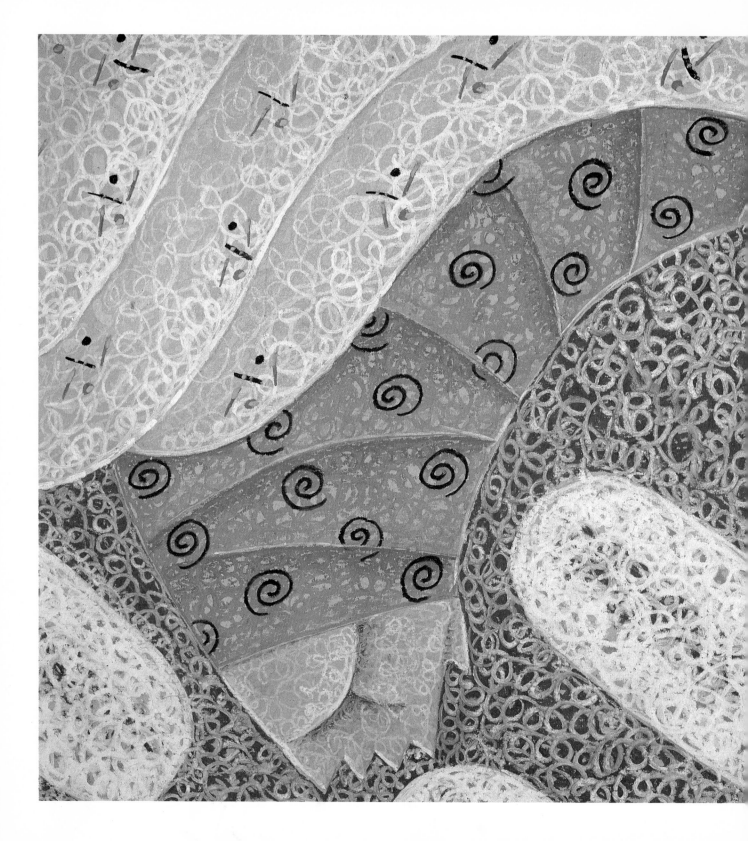

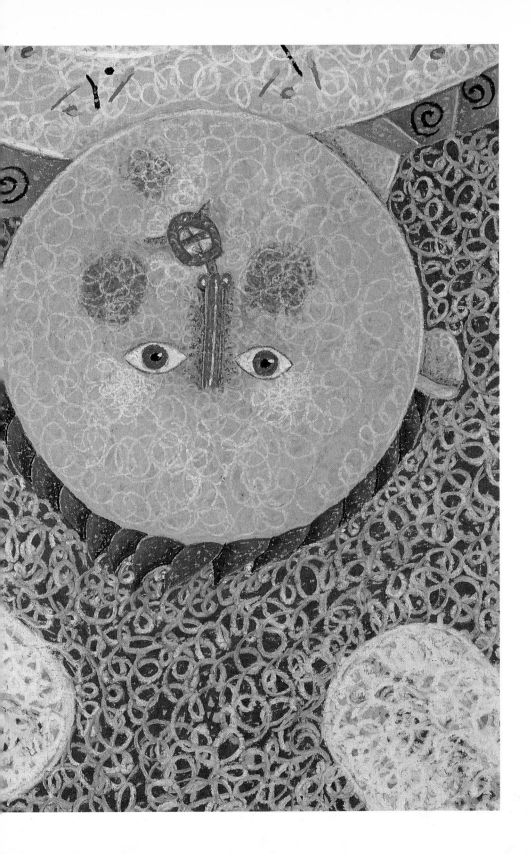

and plucked
Billy from
his bed

and bounced
him on
his head
into a camp
of cantankerous
cowboys.

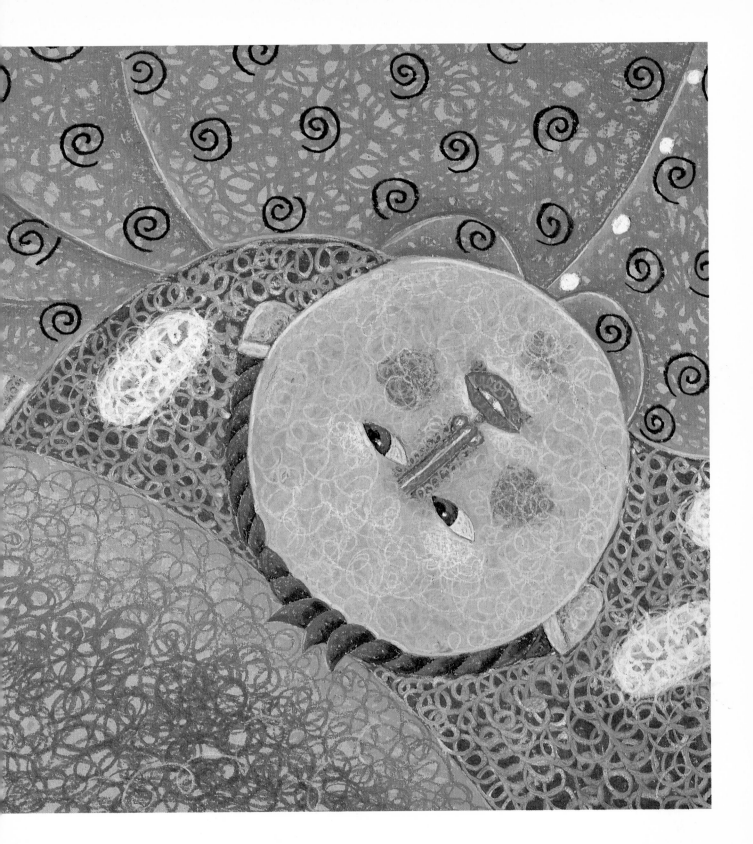

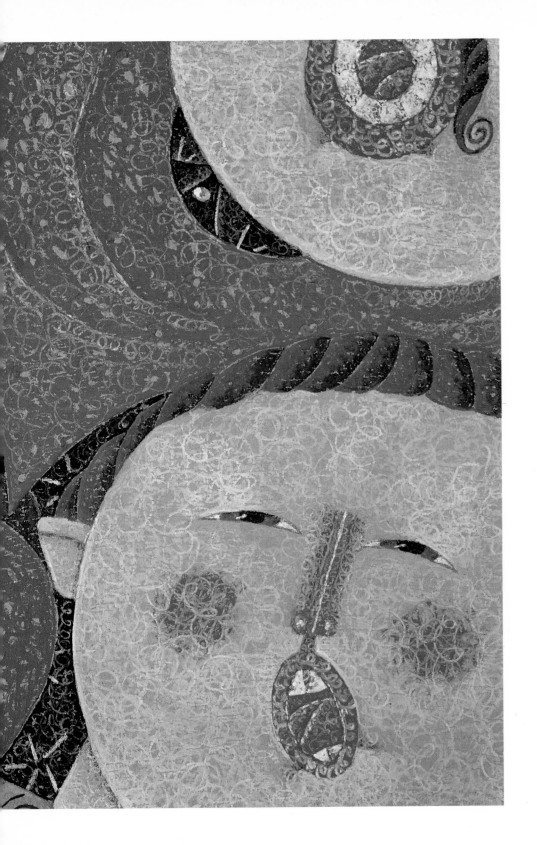

Together,
they twanged
and yelped
and hummed
and heartily
strummed.

They snatched
stars from
the sky
and sang tune
after tune

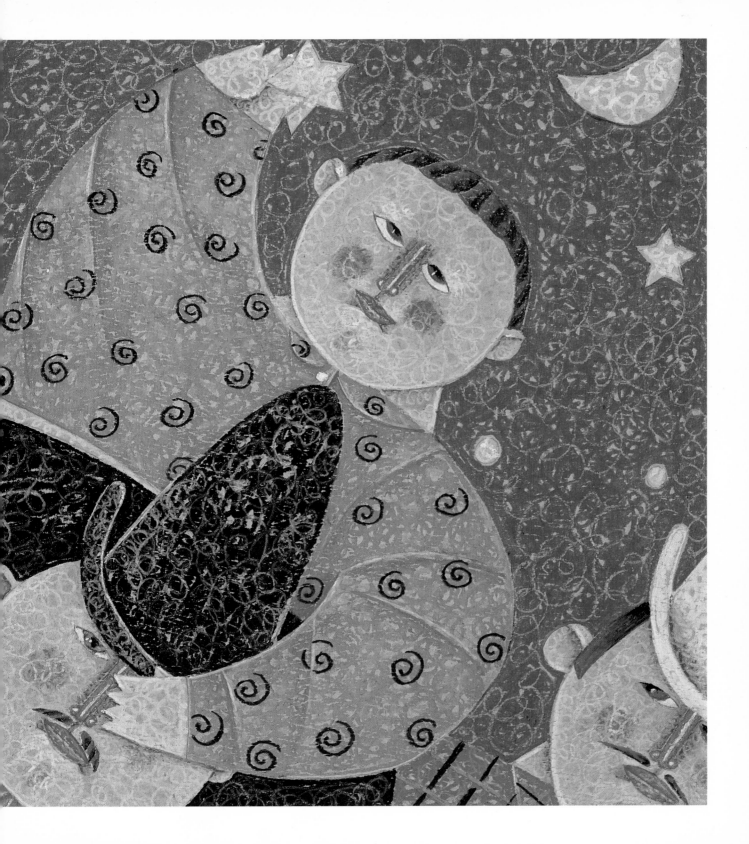

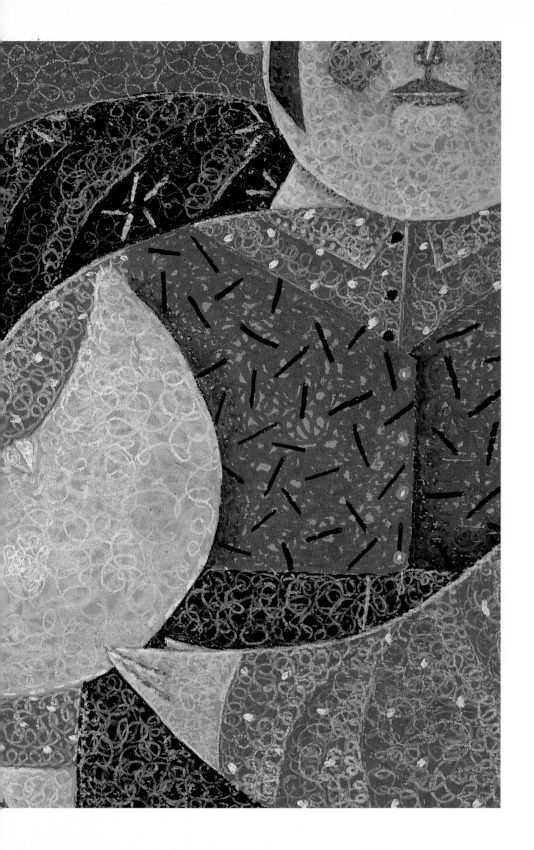

until they
ran out of stars
and lassoed
the moon.

The cowboys
clomped
and stomped
their feet and
prancing dogs
danced
to the beat,

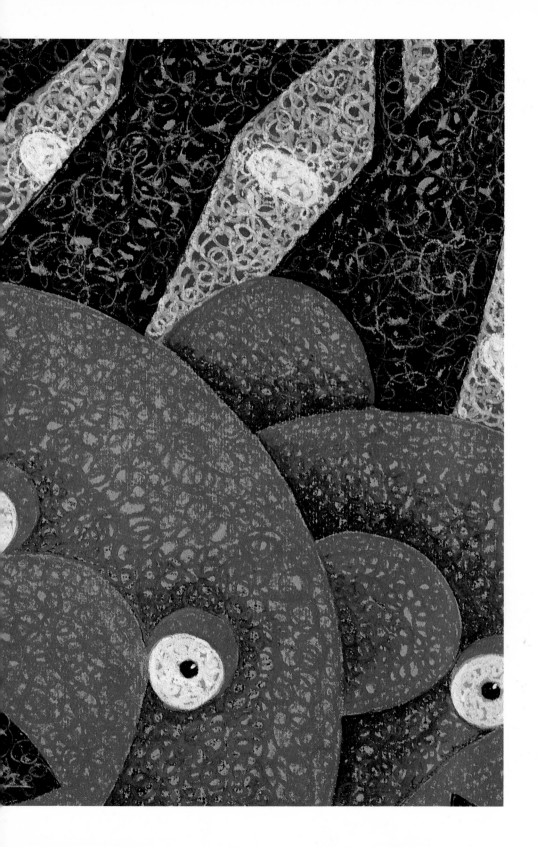

while, nearby,
grizzlies
grumbled
and growled.

Billy
climbed onto
a bronco's back,

and the
cowboys
plucked needles
from cacti
and flung them
at wolves
who were
wandering by.

Then the
howling wind
kicked up
and whirled
and swirled
and sucked Billy
into the blue,

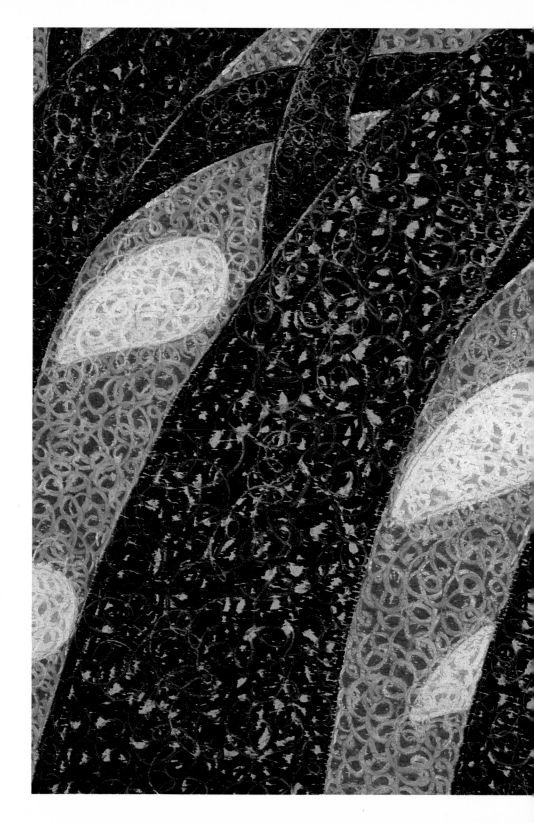

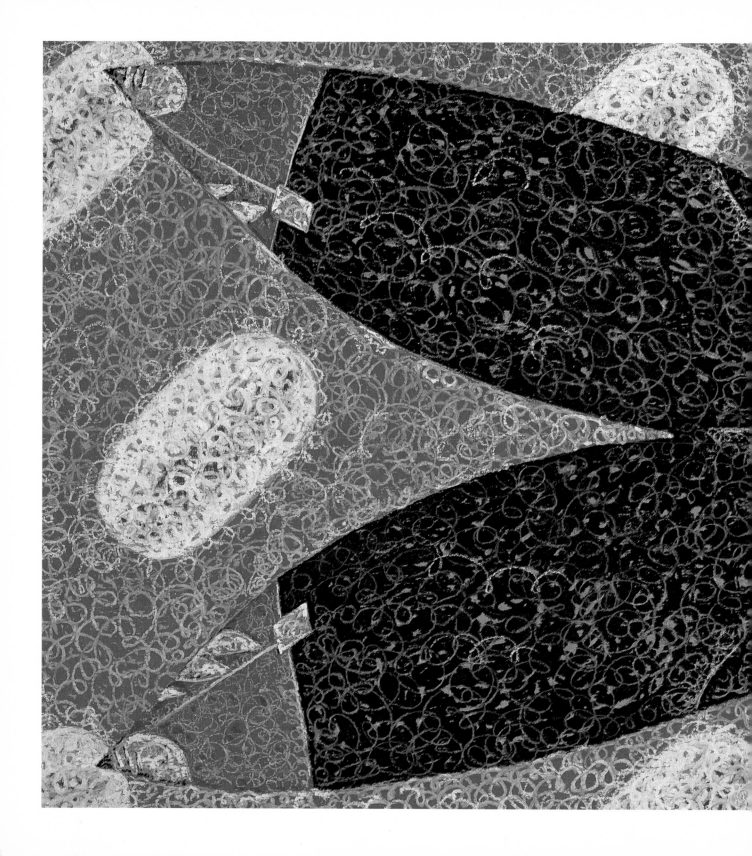

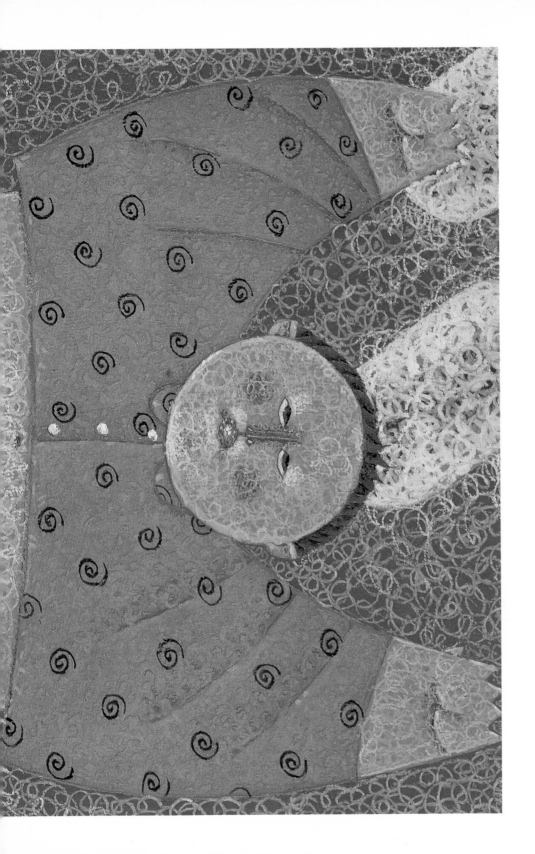

across the blue

to his home

where his mom
called, "Billy,
come in
from the blue.
I've made
rattlesnake
stew for you."